The Pride Street Crew
8
Damp Dog

Mike Wilson

Published in association with
The Basic Skills Agency

Hodder & Stoughton

Acknowledgements
Cover: Jim Eldridge
Illustrations: Jim Eldridge

Orders; please contact Bookpoint Ltd, 39 Milton Park, Abingdon, Oxon OX14 4TD. Telephone: (44) 01235 400414, Fax: (44) 01235 400454. Lines are open from 9.00–6.00, Monday to Saturday, with a 24 hour message answering service. Email address: orders@bookpoint.co.uk

British Library Cataloguing in Publication Data
A catalogue record for this title is available from the British Library

ISBN 0 340 77630 7

First published 2000
Impression number 10 9 8 7 6 5 4 3 2 1
Year   2005 2004 2003 2002 2001 2000

Copyright © 2000 Mike Wilson

Typeset by GreenGate Publishing Services, Tonbridge, Kent.
Printed in Great Britain for Hodder and Stoughton Educational, a division of Hodder Headline Plc, 338 Euston Road, London NW1 3BH, by Atheneum Press, Gateshead, Tyne & Wear

JOHN / BONE

WESLEY / TALL

LUKE / SKY

SIMON / CUSTARD

CARL / SPOT.

I am a soldier.
A soldier, strong and brave.
I am ready to die
to save the land I love.

I go up
to the top of a mountain:
the Mountain of Doom.

Then I stand and look down
on the lands below.

In my arms is a big gun.

My gun is a laser gun.
With this gun,
I have no fear.

I am ready to die
to save the land I love.

Well, no.

I'm not a soldier.
Not really.
I'm just a kid.
I go to school.

The Mountain of Doom
is not a real mountain.
I'm just going up our stairs at home.

And really,
the laser gun is Mum's hoover.

'While you're up there,' shouts Mum,
'do that room of yours.'

'That's what I *am* doing!' I shout.

Mums.
They never stop, do they?

I've got to get my room tidy.
It's Saturday night and
Lizzy is coming round tonight.

It's the first time she's seen my room.
I want it to look good.

I put all the dirty clothes in one pile.
Then I put my clean clothes in a pile.
Then I make the bed.

Some old bits of food are on the floor.
I kick them under the bed.
I get all my CDs in a pile by the wall.

Now you can see a little bit of the carpet.
I run the hoover over it
two or three times.
Lots of bits rattle up the tube.

Mum comes up,
and stands at the door.

'Well I never,' she says.
'It must be love!'

Lizzy comes round at half eight.

We go up to my room.
I kick off my trainers,
and put on a CD.

Lizzy has a good look round.

Then she folds her arms, and says:
'Well, that's got to go, for a start!'

'What?' I ask.

'That!'

My poster from the hit TV show –
Babes on the Beach.

'What's wrong with it?' I ask.
Lizzy won't say
and really,
I know what's wrong with it.

Lizzy steps up on the bed,
and pulls the poster down.

She rips it in two.
Then she opens the window,
and out goes my *Babes* poster.

Then Lizzy turns her nose up.
'What's that smell?' she says.

'What smell?' I go.
'I can't smell a thing ...'

She gets down on her knees,
and looks under the bed.

'Oh my god!'

She finds a dinner plate.
It's crusty with old food.

'You pig!' she says.

Then Lizzy reaches under the bed again.
She pulls out an old pizza box.
In the box is a fur pizza.

'Oh my god!' she says again.
'I think I'm going to be sick!'

'Who put that there?' I say.

I throw the fur pizza out the window.

'There's *still* a bad smell in here!' says Lizzy.
She sniffs and sniffs around the room,
and stops at my pile of dirty clothes.

'OK,' I say.

I go and get a bin liner.
All my clothes go out the window as well.

Lizzy is still not happy.
She still won't sit down.
She won't relax.
She turns her nose up again.

'Have you had a shower today?' she asks.
'Have you washed your feet?'

'You sound just like my mother!' I say.

'Well, have you?'

I don't answer.
There is no answer to that, is there?

'I don't want to say anything, Luke …'
says Lizzy.

I know this one.
When Lizzy says – I don't want to say anything,
it means she wants to say something.

'I don't want to say anything …' she says.
'But you need to think about …
keeping clean.

I mean – look at your hair.
Have you looked in your ears lately?
And your feet …

You remind me a bit of my grandad's dog,'
says Lizzy, 'when she's been out in the rain.'

I sit on the bed.
I hold my head in my hands.

I was really looking forward to tonight.
I was looking forward to being with Lizzy.
I was looking forward to kissing her and that.

Not any more.
She says I smell like a damp dog.

'Have a nice long bath,' says Lizzy,
'and I'll see you tomorrow.'

With that,
Lizzy walks out, and goes home.

A soldier must be strong.
A soldier must face danger and pain.

Only then
can he win the battle
for Freedom and Glory.

Only then
can he have clean feet and ears.

Next day, Lizzy came round
after her driving lesson.

She was ages talking to my mum.

I stayed in my room.
I just didn't feel like seeing anyone.

Then Lizzy comes in
and tips all this stuff on the bed.

It's bottles and bottles of …
stuff.

Stuff to put on your hair …
Stuff to put under your arms …
Stuff to put on your spots …

Bath stuff, shower stuff, smelly stuff …

(Lizzy's mum works in a shop,
and gets this stuff cheap.)

'Lizzy,' I say.
'You're not going to do
what I think you're going to do ...'

But she is.

'Right,' says Lizzy.
'Let's get to work!'

I think about saying no.
But – you don't say no to Lizzy.
Not when she's like this.

Anyway – I trust her.
Lizzy knows what she's doing –
most of the time.

So I go along with it.

Soon I am up to my ears in smelly stuff.
I'm clean and raw.
I've scraped the soft down off my chin.
I sting with after-shave.
I smell nice
in places I didn't know I had.

Lizzy has even cut my hair.
She's put highlights in it.

Highlights!
What will the Pride Street Crew think?

Two hours later,
Lizzy has done.
'Luke, you look so cool!' she says.

I look like a runaway
from the Backstreet Boys.

Lizzy and I go into town.

She says some shops
are open on Sundays.
She wants me to get some new things.

Lizzy picks a totally cool shirt,
so I buy it.

I see some cool trainers as well.
But they're £89.
I'll have to save up for a month or two.

Lizzy is being dead nice and friendly.
She's got her arm around me.
She keeps on kissing my neck.

It's not bad – being clean.
I think I might get used to it.

Just then we see two girls from school.

Lisa Hardy and Tamsin Taylor
are just coming out of the shopping centre.
They've been looking at shoes in *Feet First*.

'Hey Lizzy,' says Lisa Hardy.
'When did you dump Luke Sky?
Your new boyfriend is really good looking!'

'Wow!' says Tamsin Taylor.
'Luke, is that you?
You look ... neat.'

Lizzy laughs.
I go mega-red.

Lisa and Tamsin walk on.
They are talking, heads together.

'See,' says Lizzy.
'I'm so proud of you, Luke!'
She pulls me round
and gives me a big hug.

Over Lizzy's shoulder,
I can see Lisa and Tamsin walking away.

Tamsin turns and looks back,
and she's looking at me.

Tamsin starts to smile.
I smile back.

If you have enjoyed reading about the Pride Street Crew, you may be interested in other books in the series.